TROLLS
on Vacation

The Troll Trouble series

TROLLS
on Vacation

Alan MacDonald
Illustrated by Mark Beech

BLOOMSBURY
CHILDREN'S
BOOKS

PRIDDLES: Roger, Jackie, and Warren
Description: Pasty-faced peeples
Likes: Peace and quiet
Dislikes: Trolls

MR. TROLL: Egbert / Eggy
Description: Tall, dark,
and scaresome
Likes: Roaring, tromping,
hiding under bridges

MRS. TROLL: Nora
Description: Gorgeous
(ask Mr. Troll)
Likes: Huggles and kisses,
caves, the dark

ULRIK TROLL
Description: Big for his age
Likes: Smells, singing,
rockball

GOAT
Description:
Strong-smelling,
beardy beast
Likes: Mountains, grass
Dislikes: Being eaten

118291

For the brilliant Kate Shaw,
who believed in trolls —A. M.

To my sister Janet —M. B.

Text copyright © 2007 by Alan MacDonald
Illustrations copyright © 2007 by Mark Beech

First published in Great Britain in 2007 by Bloomsbury Publishing Plc
Published in the United States in 2008 by Bloomsbury U.S.A. Children's Books
175 Fifth Avenue, New York, New York 10010
Distributed to the trade by Macmillan

Library of Congress Cataloging-in-Publication Data
MacDonald, Alan.
Trolls on vacation / by Alan MacDonald ; illustrations by Mark Beech. — 1st U.S. ed.
p.   cm. — (Troll trouble)
Summary: When the Trolls and their neighbors, the Priddles, go off on
vacation at the same time, both families are in for some surprises.
ISBN-13: 978-1-59990-204-3 • ISBN-10: 1-59990-204-4 (hardcover)
ISBN-13: 978-1-59990-205-0 • ISBN-10: 1-59990-205-2 (paperback)
[1. Trolls—Fiction. 2. Vacations—Fiction. 3. Neighbors—Fiction.]
I. Beech, Mark, ill. II. Title.
PZ7.M145Tro 2008   [E]—dc22   2007030168

First U.S. Edition 2008
Typeset by Polly Napper/Lobster Design
Printed in the U.S.A. by Quebecor World Fairfield
2 4 6 8 10 9 7 5 3 1 (hardcover)
2 4 6 8 10 9 7 5 3 1 (paperback)

Going Shirtless

IT was a hot, sunny day at the start of the summer. At Number 10 Mountain View the Trolls were out in their backyard. Mrs. Troll lazed in a deck chair, leafing through a magazine while she cooled her hairy feet in a bowl of water. Her husband had stripped off his T-shirt and stood knee-deep in a hole that he was digging with his bare hands. Every now and then showers of earth flew in all directions. Ulrik lolled on the grass, staring at the sky. It was only three days since the end of school and he had nothing to do.

"Mom," he said.

"Yes, my ugglesome?"

"When are we going on vacation?"

"We *are* on vacation."

"Yes, but I mean *real* vacation. Where you go somewhere."

Mr. Troll paused to wipe away a drip of sweat that hung from his snout. "We could go to that stinksome hole under High Street. We haven't been there for weeks."

Ulrik shook his head. "That's a subway, Dad. I mean a proper vacation!"

Mr. Troll climbed out of his hole and wiped his hands on his gigantic belly. He looked at his wife in bemusement. "What the bogles is he talking about?"

"Ulrik's right. It's in my magazine," said Mrs. Troll. "That's what peeples do in summer—go on their vacations."

"Well, where is it then?" asked Mr. Troll.

"What?"

"This holidays you want to go on."

"How should I know? I've never gone on it!"

"Warren says it's the seasides," explained Ulrik. "You take a towel and you have to lie on it till you get really hot, then you tromp into the sea to cool down."

Mr. Troll snorted. "Makes no sense. Why get all hot and blethered just so you can get cold again? Anyway, the sea is for fishes. Trolls don't belong in the sea. Caves and forests—that's where trolls live."

"And houses," Ulrik pointed out. "We live in a house."

"Yes, well, houses as well," agreed Mr. Troll. "Caves and forests and houses."

"But couldn't we go on a vacation, Dad? We've never been!"

Mrs. Troll lifted her feet out of the bowl and waggled her toes.

"It might be nice, Eggy. Why don't we?"

"But I've just started making a wading pool!" objected Mr. Troll, pointing at the muddy hole he had dug.

"You can finish it when we come back."

"Please, Dad!" begged Ulrik. "Can we?"

Mr. Troll sighed and picked up his shirt. It was covered in dirt, but he didn't mind since it had been pretty filthy in the first place. "We'll see," he said. He studied the cover of Mrs. Troll's magazine, which showed a sandy beach crowded with hundreds of people who seemed to be wearing only their underwear.

"Hmm," he said. "So how do you get to this seasides?"

Ulrik didn't know. He'd never been to the sea. In fact, he'd never been much farther than High Street. He'd been to Troll Mountain, of course—that's where they used to live before they moved to Biddlesden—but there was no sea back home, only mountains, forests, and gray mist. He didn't know how far it was to the seasides. Could you walk there or did you have to catch a bus?

Mrs. Troll had been thinking. "What about that shop on High Street, Eggy? The Trouble Agents. I'm sure they do vacations."

Mr. Troll looked puzzled. "You want to stay in a shop?"

"No," said Mrs. Troll. "You ask the Trouble Agent and he finds you a vacation. It's like the supermarket, only without the cornflakes."

"Oh," said Mr. Troll. "Well, if you want we can try it tomorrow."

Next door, Mrs. Priddle stared out of her kitchen window while she chopped up carrots with more force than was strictly necessary.

"Look at him!" she tutted. "It's disgusting!"

"What is?" asked her son, Warren, hurrying over to look.

"That Mr. Troll. Parading around in nothing but a tiny pair of shorts. As if I want to see that before my dinner!"

"What's wrong with it? Dad sometimes wears shorts," Warren pointed out.

"Yes, but he's not a troll. Look at the size of that belly. The least he could do is cover it up."

Warren stood on a chair to get a better look at Mr. Troll's belly. It was true—it was impressively big. Warren had seen Mr. Troll's belly before, bulging beneath the filthy T-shirt he always wore, but today it was on display to the world. It was pale green, with a forest of coarse dark hair that spread from his chest to his belly button. When Mr. Troll walked, his belly wobbled like Jell-O. Warren thought you could hold a party on it. If Mr. Troll lay on his back, you could use him as a bouncy castle.

The front door slammed.

"Roger, is that you? Come and see this!" called Mrs. Priddle.

Mr. Priddle came in humming to himself happily and planted a kiss on his wife's cheek.

"See what, my darling?" he asked.

"That!" said Mrs. Priddle, pointing next door. "Can you believe it?"

"Oh! He's not digging holes again, is he?"

"It's not the holes that worry me," said Mrs. Priddle. "Look what he's wearing!"

Mr. Priddle peered out of the window. "Shorts," he said.

"He's practically naked! I've never seen anything so horrible in all my life."

"Well, don't look," said Mr. Priddle.

"This is my kitchen, Roger. I'll look where I want. I'm not going to go around with my eyes shut just because that ugly brute can't be bothered to wear a

T-shirt! This could go on all summer. Before we know it they'll all be parading around the garden in their underwear!"

"Ugh! Mom!" said Warren, pulling a face.

"Well, aren't you going to speak to him?" demanded Mrs. Priddle.

"You're the one who's offended. You speak to him," replied Mr. Priddle.

"How can I speak to him? He's not wearing a T-shirt!"

"Never mind his shirt!" said Mr. Priddle. "I've got something to show you. Both of you. Come out to the front."

"Why?" asked Mrs. Priddle suspiciously.

"You'll see. It's a surprise."

Mrs. Priddle groaned. "Oh, Roger, you know I hate surprises!"

Mr. Priddle forced his wife and son to shut their eyes and, holding them by the arm, he led them outside.

"All right. You can look now."

They both opened their eyes. "Oh, my giddy bananas!" gasped Mrs. Priddle.

"It's a camper," said Mr. Priddle.

"I can see that, Roger. But what's it doing in our driveway?"

"It's ours!" said Mr. Priddle proudly. "I bought it."

The camper was the color of old chicken soup. It had lace curtains at the windows that might have been white a hundred years ago.

Warren thought it was fantastic. "Can we look inside?" he asked eagerly.

"Of course!" said Mr. Priddle. "Just be careful with the light switch—it needs fixing."

He took them on a tour. It didn't take too long, since the camper had only three rooms—a tiny bedroom, a tinier bathroom, and a kitchen-slash-dining-slash-everything-else room.

"See?" said Mr. Priddle. "You fold away the table like this and you've got another bed."

"And who's going to sleep on that?" asked Mrs. Priddle, folding her arms.

"Well, us," said Mr. Priddle. "When we're on vacation."

Mrs. Priddle pursed her lips. "If you think I'm going on vacation in this, you're mistaken—"

"I like it, Dad!" shouted Warren from next door, where he was using the bed as a trampoline.

"You promised me we'd have a real vacation this year," said Mrs. Priddle.

"And we will. What could be more fun than a camper?"

"A hotel," said Mrs. Priddle. "A five-star hotel with a view of the sea. And a swimming pool."

"Yes, but—"

"And cooked breakfast!" shouted Warren from next door. "Sausage, bacon, and eggs!"

"Be quiet, Warren!" ordered Mr. Priddle. "Anyway, we can have all those things—the view, the swimming pool—they'll all be at the campground."

Mrs. Priddle narrowed her eyes. "What campground?"

"Um . . . well . . . ," Mr. Priddle stammered, "I mean, if we found one we liked."

"Roger," warned Mrs. Priddle, "if you've done something stupid, I'm going to scream."

Mr. Priddle dug in his pocket and pulled out a scrap of paper. This wasn't going as well as he'd hoped. "It's not a campsite," he said, "it's more of a farm, really. I found the ad in *Caravan and Camping*."

His wife snatched the paper from him and read it out loud.

Paradise View
Find paradise by a sun-kissed sea.
Sea views, natural swimming pool, tennis court—
everything for a vacation you'll never forget.
Campers welcome. Pets and children extra.
Phone: Olwen Ogwen—Boggy Moor 657770

"Olwen Ogwen?" said Mrs. Priddle. "What kind of a name is that?"

"He's European. Sounded like a nice guy on the phone."

"You've spoken to him already?"

"Well, yes, I had to . . . when I, um . . . booked the vacation."

Mrs. Priddle let out a piercing scream and kicked the folding bed. There was a twang as it collapsed.

"Don't worry," said Mr. Priddle, "that can be fixed."

The Joy of Camping

T HE next morning, the Trolls trooped into town to visit the travel agents.

The sales assistant who greeted them was named Kelly. Ulrik knew this because she had a name badge on her bright blue jacket. She had very white teeth and bright pink nails and smelled like perfume. Ulrik moved his chair a bit closer to the desk so he could smell her better. He was curious about peeple's smells. Most trolls smelled much the same—mainly of dirt and sweat and goat meat, if that's what they'd had for breakfast—but Ulrik had noticed peeples had different smells. Babies, for instance, smelled of sour milk while old ladies smelled of mints.

Kelly smiled with her dazzling white teeth. "How can I help?"

"We want to go on a vacation," said Mrs. Troll.

"No problem," smiled Kelly. "What kind of vacation did you have in mind?"

"Well, not a subway," said Mrs. Troll. "We've been to one of those."

"We want somewhere with mountains," said Mr. Troll.

"And the seasides," nodded Ulrik.

"Towels, too. It's got to have towels," added Mrs. Troll.

Kelly's smile had faded and she was looking slightly confused. "Towels?" she said.

"Yes, to sit on. We don't want sand on our bottoms."

"Well, no," agreed Kelly. "But generally most people take their own towels."

Mrs. Troll shook her head firmly. "We don't have any."

"No," said Mr. Troll. "Trolls never wash—it takes away your stink."

Kelly laughed, hoping this was a joke. They seemed to have gone on to a new subject.

"So you're interested in the beach?" she said.

"Is that at the seasides?" asked Mrs. Troll.

"Well, yes, most beaches are."

"Then that's what we want."

"No problem, we've got plenty of choices. Have you thought where you'd like to go? Spain? California? The Greek Islands?"

"That sounds good. Can we walk there?" asked Mr. Troll.

"Which?"

"The Goat Islands."

"Um . . . Greek Islands. Not really. You'd need to fly."

Mr. Troll snorted. "We're trolls, not ducky birds. How can we fly?"

Kelly glanced behind them. A line of people were waiting.

"You don't have to go abroad," she said. "There

are plenty of options at home. Where would you like to stay? In a hotel?"

Mr. Troll leaned forward. "What about a cave?"

"A cave?"

"Yes, we'd like that," agreed Mrs. Troll. "A nice stinksome cave."

Kelly shook her head. "I don't think we have any, um, cave vacations. If you want something cheaper, why don't you try camping or perhaps renting a camper?"

"A what?"

"That's what Warren's talking about!" said Ulrik eagerly. "He told me his dad's bought a camper and they're going to the seasides."

"That sounds nice, Eggy," said Mrs. Troll.

Kelly was busy tapping on her computer keyboard.

"What about this?" she said. "Two weeks at Golden Sands Park in a luxury camper."

"Luxury, Eggy, think of that!" said Mrs. Troll.

"Uggsome!" said Ulrik. "Can we go, Dad?"

Mr. Troll considered. "Does it have a wading pool or do we have to dig our own?"

Kelly consulted her screen. "Let's see . . . there's an outdoor swimming pool."

"Then we'll go," said Mr. Troll. He'd had enough digging for one week.

Kelly tapped again. "Lovely. That will be $599 if you go before August."

The Trolls looked shocked. None of them had considered they might have to pay for a vacation. They assumed that travel agents were giving them away. Mrs. Troll reached into her bag and brought out the sock she used as a wallet. She

peered inside—they definitely didn't have that much money.

"Let's talk to the Priddles," she suggested. "They've got a camper."

"So you don't want to book?" asked Kelly.

"No, thanks," said Mr. Troll. "Maybe we'll come back tomorrow."

"Of course." Kelly stood up and smiled with relief. Tomorrow was Sunday and luckily they were closed.

Later that evening, Mrs. Priddle happened to glance out of her bedroom window.

"Roger!" she called downstairs. "You better get outside. Mrs. Troll's looking at your camper."

"Oh, good gravy!" Mr. Priddle cried and hurried outside in his slippers. He found Mrs. Troll with her snout jammed up against the back window.

"What do you think? A beauty, isn't she? I only picked her up yesterday," said Mr. Priddle, modestly patting the side of his camper.

"Has it got towels?" asked Mrs. Troll.

"Well, yes, it's got everything," said Mr. Priddle. "Want to have a look inside?"

Mrs. Troll did. The camper was a little on the small side and she had to duck low to fit through the door, but once inside she was enchanted with the cozy little room. Mr. Priddle took her around, pointing out the stove, the fridge-freezer, the shower, and all the modern gadgets the camper had to offer. Mrs. Troll was especially impressed with the table that magically turned into a bed.

"So what do you think?" asked Mr. Priddle.

"It's stinksome," said Mrs. Troll.

"Well, yes, I know it could do with a good clean."

"No, don't spoil it. It's got a lovely stink."

"Oh, well, thanks," said Mr. Priddle.

"And you're going in this for your vacation?"

"Yes, we're off bright and early tomorrow to miss the traffic. It's quite a journey to the sea."

"Yes, it's a long walk." Mrs. Troll nodded wisely. She looked around the camper enviously. "Ulrik has been begging us for a vacation, poor hairling. I wish we had a camper."

"Well, you should try it," said Mr. Priddle.

"Me?" said Mrs. Troll.

"All of you. There's nothing to beat it. Go where you like, stay as long you please—with a camper, you're free as a bird. Who needs an expensive hotel when you've got everything you need right here?"

Mrs. Troll had never thought of it that way before. "Maybe you're right."

"I am right. You should give it some thought," urged Mr. Priddle.

"Well, I will—if you're sure."

"Sure? I'm positive! I think you'd love it."

"All right. Thank you. I'll see what Eggy thinks."

Mrs. Troll's dark eyes were shining with delight and she suddenly hugged her neighbor.

Mr. Priddle watched her go. She had seemed really impressed with the camper, though he had a nagging sense that they'd been talking about different things. What had she meant when she'd asked him if he was sure? Sure of what? He'd only meant they ought to consider buying a camper of their own. So why had she acted as if he was doing them an enormous favor?

Mrs. Priddle was waiting for her husband in the kitchen. "Well, what did she want?"

"Nothing, really—just a look around. Actually, we had a nice chat. Very interested in the camper."

"Huh!" snorted Mrs. Priddle. "When you live in a pigsty, anything looks good."

"They're actually very friendly if you give them a chance," said Mr. Priddle.

Mrs. Priddle clicked her tongue. "Don't be ridiculous, Roger," she said. "The best thing about

going away is we won't have to see them for two whole weeks."

Next door at Number 10, Mrs. Troll had reported the conversation to her husband.

"Are you sure?" he said.

"Of course I am, Eggy. He wants us to go on vacation with them!"

"Blunking bogles!" said Mr. Troll. "What did he say?"

"He said we should try it, all of us. He thinks we'd love it."

Ulrik came into the kitchen. "Love what, Mom?"

"A camper vacation, hairling," said Mrs. Troll. "The Priddles have asked us to go with them."

"Uggsome!" said Ulrik. "Are we going?"

Mrs. Troll looked at Mr. Troll. "What do you think? Should we, Eggy?"

Mr. Troll picked at one of his fangs. "Won't it be a little squished? Six of us together in that tiddly tin can?"

"It's bigger inside than you'd think," said Mrs. Troll. "It's got a table that turns into a bed. Why don't we, Eggy? No one's ever asked us on vacation before."

Mr. Troll thought it over. It was true they didn't have a camper and the Priddles had a perfectly good one. This way it wouldn't cost them any money, either.

"All right," he said. "We'll go!"

Ulrik gave a loud whoop and threw himself on his dad, wrestling him to the ground. A mock fight broke out, with the two of them growling and laughing.

Mrs. Troll left them to it and bustled upstairs. If they were going to leave early in the morning, she'd have to start packing. In fact, there was hardly any point in going to bed. An idea struck her. Why not give the Priddles a lovely surprise? They could move into the camper tonight so they'd be all ready for the early start in the morning. She couldn't wait to see the look on Mr. Priddle's face when he opened the door.

Paradise View

THE trolls slept soundly through the journey, lulled by the sound of cars on the highway. They were still dozing when the camper pulled into a driveway by a signpost that said "Paradise View." The camper rocked from side to side as it climbed a potholed track to the top of a hill. Mr. Priddle parked and turned off the engine. He peered through the steady drizzle outside.

"Is this it?" asked Mrs. Priddle. "Where are all the other campers?"

The Priddles got out and looked around, huddled under a golfing umbrella. Even Mr. Priddle had to admit that Paradise View fell short of what he was expecting. A few sheep grazed in a field of scrubby grass. There was one rusty faucet, a barn with a rickety roof, a grim-looking farmhouse, and not much else. Crows cawed in the woods behind them. A man came out of the farmhouse and strode toward them with two sheepdogs trotting at his heels.

"Ah," said Mr. Priddle. "This will be Ogwen."

"Tell him," his wife hissed. "Tell him we don't want to stay."

Farmer Ogwen stepped over a puddle. He had a face like a knobbly red potato. His corduroys were tied at the waist with string and tucked into his muddy boots. Warren thought he looked more like a tramp than the owner of a campsite.

The two dogs circled them, growling softly. "Quiet, Fang! Down, Claw!" Ogwen barked. He smiled, revealing his two remaining teeth, and held out a grubby hand. "Olwen Ogwen. Don't worry about the dogs—they won't hurt you. Quiet, boys! Quiet, I said!"

The dogs ceased their growling but Warren kept close to the camper just in case.

"You must be Widdle," said the farmer. "You found us all right, then?"

"Yes. It's Priddle. Roger Priddle."

"Oh, right. So you're on your vacation, are you? You'll like it here. Paradise on earth."

"It's more like the end of the earth," muttered Mrs. Priddle.

"Eh?" demanded Ogwen.

Standing close to the camper, Warren could hear strange noises coming from inside.

"Dad!" he said.

"Not now, Warren—I'm talking. I was wondering, Mr. Ogwen, where are all the other campers?"

"Oh. Too early in the season," said the farmer. "This will be packed in a couple of weeks. They'll be lining up right along the lane."

Mrs. Priddle tried to imagine the bare field crowded with happy vacationers, but it was asking a lot of her imagination.

Mr. Priddle looked around. "The ad . . . ," he began.

"You saw that, did you? Wrote that myself," said Ogwen.

"But it mentioned a swimming pool. I can't see it."

Farmer Ogwen pointed to the bottom of the hill. "Down there—look. By the reeds."

"That's a pond," said Mrs. Priddle, squinting into the rain.

"Yes, natural pool. Beautiful on a hot day. The cows love it."

Mrs. Priddle turned pale. "Roger, say something," she muttered.

"Um . . . ," said Mr. Priddle.

Warren, meanwhile, was listening. There was definitely something moving in the camper. Bumps and thumps and scrapes came from inside. "Dad!" he said again.

"Not now, Warren!" snapped Mr. Priddle. "And the tennis court? Where's that?"

"Oh, that went last year. Sheep kept eating the grass. And there's the problem of droppings, see? Can't stop sheep doing what's natural, can you?"

Mrs. Priddle gave a faint moan.

"But the view," her husband plowed on. "Your ad promised a sea view."

"Well, there is!" smiled Ogwen, showing his two teeth. "If you climb the hill on a clear day, you can see it across the bog. Of course it's not clear now—it's raining. Always rains on Boggy Moor." He clapped his hands together. "So, if that's all, I'll leave you to get settled in, shall I?"

He turned to go, but a loud knocking sound caught his attention.

"Someone in your camper, is there?"

Mr. Priddle glanced at his wife. "No."

"That's what I keep telling you!" said Warren. "There *is* something. Listen!"

They all stood and listened. A loud thump came from inside the camper and Mr. Priddle took a step back. The handle of the door rattled as if someone was trying to get out. Mrs. Priddle looked as if she might faint. They had been traveling for hours, they had come to a place run by a toothless madman—and now this.

"Better open the door, hadn't you?" said Ogwen.

Mr. Priddle took a deep breath. He unlocked the door, turned the handle, and leaped backward as if he were releasing a caged lion. A hairy head appeared, blinking at them. Mr. Troll was wearing his red Bermuda shorts and nothing else.

"Ah, Piddle," he said, scratching under his arms. "What's for breakfast?"

Mr. Troll stepped out of the camper into the drizzly rain, followed by Ulrik. Mrs. Troll came next, wearing a flowing pink nightgown, trimmed with silk bows.

"My stars!" said Ogwen. "How many have you got in there?"

Mrs. Priddle glared at her husband. "Don't look at me!" said Mr. Priddle. "I had no idea!"

Ulrik was looking around. He had been expecting a sandy beach with waves lapping on the shore, but all he could see was a muddy field and a dozen sheep. He tugged at his mom's arm. "Where's the seasides, Mom?"

"Never mind that!" said Mrs. Priddle. "What on earth are you doing here?"

Mrs. Troll looked mystified. "We're on vacation, just like you."

"But you can't just show up! You can't just move into our camper, uninvited!"

"We *were* invited," replied Mr. Troll. "He invited us." He pointed a fat finger at Mr. Priddle.

Mrs. Priddle turned on her husband. "Roger! You didn't!"

"Of course I didn't!"

"Don't tell fibwoppers. You did!" said Mrs. Troll.

"No, I didn't!"

"Oh yes, you did!"

"Don't stop!" grinned Ogwen. "This is better than charades."

"You said we should try a camper vacation. You told me we'd love it," said Mrs. Troll.

"Yes, but I didn't mean that you should come on vacation with *us*!"

"Didn't you?"

"No!"

"Then why did you invite us?"

Mr. Priddle gave up—they were going around in

circles. He should have known something like this would happen. It seemed the Trolls followed them around like bad luck.

"Well, this is marvelous," said Mrs. Priddle bitterly. "Just wonderful!"

"Isn't it?" said Mr. Troll, beaming. "All of us together! On vacation."

Farmer Ogwen had been making calculations. "So there's six of you," he said. "You said only three on the phone. I'm afraid six is going to be extra."

Mrs. Priddle jumped to her feet. This was the last straw. "There are *not* six of us," she said. "There is only room in this camper for three."

"Well, that's what I said," agreed Mr. Troll. "So where are *you* going to sleep?"

Later that evening, the Priddles sat around the table inside the camper, drinking mugs of hot chocolate. Warren wiped the mist from the window beside him and looked out.

"They're still there," he said.

"What are they doing?" asked Mr. Priddle.

"Getting wet."

Mr. Priddle glanced pitifully at his wife. "Don't look at me like that," she said. "There isn't any room."

"But we can't leave them out there all night, Jackie. They'll catch their death of colds."

"You should have thought of that before you invited them."

"For the last time, I didn't invite them!" cried Mr. Priddle. "It was all a mistake."

Mrs. Priddle glared back. "If you ask me, this entire vacation was a mistake. This place should carry a health warning. I can't walk out the door without stepping in sheep poop, and as for that so-called swimming pool, the only things swimming in there are frogs and lizards!"

Warren kept his nose pressed against the window. "Do you think they *will* catch their death of colds?" he asked.

"Warren!"

"I'm only asking. It might get chilly tonight."

"They're trolls," said Mrs. Priddle. "They're used to the cold."

There was a silence. Mrs. Priddle drained the last of her hot chocolate. Warren and Mr. Priddle gazed at her reproachfully. The rain fell harder, drumming on the roof.

"Oh, go and get them," sighed Mrs. Priddle. "I must be out of my mind."

"I'll tell them," said Mr. Priddle. He took the golf umbrella and went outside.

The Trolls came in and stood by the door. Rain dripped off them, collecting in puddles at their feet.

"Thank you," said Mr. Troll, shaking himself like a dog.

"It's only for one night," warned Mrs. Priddle. "You'd better get out of those wet clothes."

"Good idea," said Mr. Troll, pulling off his soggy T-shirt.

"Not here!" shouted Mrs. Priddle. "Go in the bathroom and change. I'm afraid you'll all have to squash in one bed."

"That's all right," said Mrs. Troll. "We're used to squishing. We can squish in with you if you like."

Mrs. Priddle shuddered. "Please, no! Just go to bed. Maybe in the morning we'll find this was all a nightmare."

The Trolls retired and before long the only sound to be heard was the rumbling of Mr. Troll's snores. Ulrik lay awake listening to the rain pattering on the roof. Vacations were very different from what he'd imagined. You seemed to spend a lot of time arguing and getting wet. Still, tomorrow was a new day; maybe if it stopped raining, they'd go to the seaside.

Painting Sheep

THE next day, the clouds had blown away and the sun shone in a clear, blue sky.

After a breakfast of scrambled eggs and burnt toast (Mr. Priddle said the grill needed fixing), Ulrik and Warren asked if they could go off to explore by themselves.

The two of them wandered down the hill past the woods where the crows called to them. Ulrik could see Boggy Moor emerging from the morning mist. It looked wild and deserted, a bit like Troll Mountain, though obviously without the mountain.

"Let's play Hide and Seek," Warren suggested.

"Is that the same as Roar and Seek?" asked Ulrik. "I used to play that with my friends."

"It's easy peasy. I hide and you've got to find me."

"And when do you roar?"

"You don't roar!" said Warren impatiently. "There's no roaring in this game, okay?"

"Okay. But how am I supposed to find you?"

Warren rolled his eyes. "Look, it isn't complicated. You just close your eyes, count to fifty, then come and look for me. Got it?"

"Yes," said Ulrik. "Where will you be?"

"Arghhh!" cried Warren.

Ulrik frowned. "I thought you said there wasn't any roaring."

"Just shut your eyes and count!"

Ulrik did as he was told and counted to fifty out loud. When he opened his eyes he was alone. He scanned the hill, trying to guess where Warren would have gone. Apart from the barn and the woods, there weren't many places to hide. He decided to try the barn first.

Pushing open the door, he breathed in the sweet smell of straw and mud. It smelled a bit like

their house on Mountain View Street. At the far
end of the barn someone was bending over, sur-
rounded by sheep.

"Found you!" cried Ulrik.

But when the person turned around, it wasn't
Ulrik. It was Farmer Ogwen, who gave him a gap-
toothed smile. He was wearing the same shabby
clothes as yesterday and he'd forgotten to shave.

"Hello," said Ulrik. "I was looking for Warren. Have you seen him?"

"Not in here."

"We're playing Hide and Sneak. I've got to find him but roaring's not allowed."

Ogwen raised one bushy eyebrow. "Just as well. You might have scared me."

Ulrik shrugged modestly. "Dad says my roar's getting fiercer. I'm taking lessons."

"Good for you."

Ulrik decided he liked Ogwen's soft, sing-song way of talking. Most people he met for the first time backed away as if he was going to bite them, but Ogwen seemed quite at ease. He went back to coloring one of the sheep with the blue marker in his hand.

"Aren't they supposed to be white?" asked Ulrik.

"What's that?"

"Sheeps. You're coloring them blue."

The farmer chuckled to himself. "Oh, not blue all over. That's my mark, see? If the sheep gets lost and anyone finds it, they'll see that blue mark and they'll know she belongs to me."

"Oh, I see! Like my soccer socks," said Ulrik.

"Are they blue?"

"No, they're red, but they've got my name inside, so peeples at school know they're mine."

Ogwen nodded. "Same thing. Sheep are like socks, always getting lost." He gave Ulrik a wink. "You want to give me a hand?"

Ulrik nodded. He liked coloring. They did it at school, though mostly on paper rather than sheep. Ogwen showed him how to make a large spot on the sheep's fleece using the blue marker. Once he got the hang of it, he did several more. Some of the

sheep had red spots, which Ogwen explained was a mistake that needed to be corrected. Ulrik was so involved in what he was doing that he didn't notice Warren had come into the barn.

"Ulrik! I thought you were coming to look for me," he complained.

Ulrik swung round. "Oh, sorry, Warren. I forgot."

"It's my fault," said Ogwen. "He's been helping me."

Warren leaned on the side of the pen sulkily. "I've been waiting for hours. You never would have seen me. I found this great place in the woods."

Ogwen looked up sharply. "The woods?"

"Yes," said Warren. "Why?"

"You don't want to go there. It's close to the moor. I should have warned you."

"What's wrong with the moor?" asked Ulrik.

"Wrong? Surely you know about Boggy Moor?"

They both shook their heads. Ogwen beckoned them over with a grimy finger and lowered his voice. "There's things that happen on the moor, boys—bad things. No one goes there, not after dark. You take my advice."

"Why?" asked Warren in an awed whisper. "Why don't they go there?"

The farmer shook his head. "Take it from me, it's not safe. You keep away from the moor. Keep away."

He shook a bony finger in warning and then turned back to his sheep.

"What do you think he meant?" asked Ulrik as they left the barn.

"I don't know," said Warren. "He's probably just pulling our leg. Trying to scare us."

"Yes," said Ulrik. "Probably." He glanced back at the woods and the bleak moor beyond.

"Anyway, I'm not scared," said Warren.

"Me neither," agreed Ulrik. The camper was in sight now and they broke into a run.

Swimming Lessons

MR. PRIDDLE said that, since the sun was shining, they should spend the day on the beach. He had hoped the Trolls might have other plans, but it turned out they had no plans at all.

The six of them squashed into the Priddles' car, with Warren reluctantly forced to sit on Mrs. Troll's lap since he was the smallest. Once at the beach parking lot, they unloaded their bags, sand pails, and shovels and followed the steep path down to Sunny Bay.

Down at the beach, Ulrik noticed that everyone stopped what they were doing to stare at the Trolls. Shouts and laughter died away on the air. People drew back to let them through, pointing and whispering among themselves.

Mr. Priddle set down his bags by some rocks.

"Let's stop here," he suggested. "The tide's coming in."

A little girl ran past and stopped in front of Ulrik. She pointed a chubby finger.

"Dad! Dad! It's the big bad beast!"

Ulrik bent down to give her his friendliest smile, but before he could say anything, the girl's dad came running and gathered her up in his arms.

Looking around, Ulrik saw people were beginning to desert the beach. Some gathered up their belongings while others panicked and simply left their towels and mats behind as they fled. Within five minutes of their arrival, the beach was empty except for the Trolls and the Priddles.

Mrs. Troll stared open-mouthed. "What's wrong with everyone?"

"It's you!" said Mrs. Priddle. "Didn't you see the way they looked at you?"

"Well, haven't they seen trolls before?"

"Of course they haven't! This isn't the mountains."

"But we weren't trying to fright anyone," said Mr. Troll. "I haven't roared once."

Mr. Priddle looked up and down the deserted beach. "Well, it looks like we've got the place to ourselves. We might as well enjoy it."

He began to set up the umbrella, hammering the pole into the sand while his wife spread out three beach towels. Once this was done, the Trolls watched in surprise as the Priddles began to undress, stripping off their tops and shorts.

Mrs. Priddle caught them staring. "Aren't you getting changed?"

"Are we, Mom?" asked Ulrik.

"If you want, my ugglesome," said Mrs. Troll. "Maybe we should."

She began unbuttoning the flowery summer dress she was wearing. Mr. Troll shrugged and tugged his grubby T-shirt over his head. He unzipped his shorts and kicked them off. He was about to take off his underwear when Mrs. Priddle stopped him.

"WAIT!" she screamed, turning pink. "Aren't you wearing swim trunks?"

"Trunks?" said Mr. Troll. He looked at his wife. "Have we got trunks?"

"I don't think so, Eggy."

"Then what are you going to wear?" demanded Mrs. Priddle.

"Same as you. We'll go bareskin," said Mrs. Troll, stepping out of her dress.

"Bareskin? You can't walk around naked!" said Mrs. Priddle. "This is a beach—people are looking!"

"No, they aren't. All the peeples ran away," said Mr. Troll.

"Well, I am a peeples . . . I mean, a person," said Mrs. Priddle. "And if you haven't got swimsuits, at least keep some clothes on!"

Mr. Troll sighed and bent down to pick up his shorts. There was no pleasing peeples, he thought. First they told you to take off your clothes, then they wanted you to put them back on. In any case he couldn't see what all the fuss was about. Back home, trolls went bareskin all the time.

Mrs. Priddle had settled herself on her towel and was rubbing some kind of cream on her legs. Mrs.

Troll watched enviously. She didn't have a towel to sit on and she didn't have any cream. She sat down next to Mrs. Priddle and sniffed her legs. The cream smelled nice, like canned peaches.

"Isn't there somewhere else you could sit?" asked Mrs. Priddle, coldly.

"I haven't got a towel," said Mrs. Troll.

"Of course not. No towels, no swimsuits—anything else you didn't bring?"

"Legs cream," said Mrs. Troll, pointing at the tube in Mrs. Priddle's hand.

"It's called sunscreen. You put it on to stop from burning."

"Are you burning?" Mrs. Troll looked above Mrs. Priddle's head, checking for signs of smoke.

"No, because I always wear sunscreen. I've got delicate skin," said Mrs. Priddle, smoothing back her blonde hair. She sighed wearily. "Look, if you want some, there's another tube in the bag."

Mrs. Troll rummaged in the Priddles' picnic bag. Under the sandwiches and chips she found a large yellow tube that she assumed was the spare sunscreen. She squeezed a blob onto her hand. It was thick and yellow, though it didn't smell of peaches. She began to rub it onto her arms. "Eggy!" she said. "Can you rub some of this on my back?"

"What for?" asked Mr. Troll.

"It's sunscreen—it stops you from burning. You should try some."

Mr. Troll sniffed the tube and made a face. "Smells like eggs," he said. He squeezed out a large blob and began to rub it onto his wife's hairy back. Warren, in the meantime, had changed into his swimsuit and was waiting impatiently.

"Are you ready, Dad? I want to go for a swim!"

Mr. Priddle groaned. "Not yet! I just sat down."

Mrs. Priddle lay back on her beach towel and opened her book. "Go and swim with him, Roger. The water looks lovely."

Ulrik looked. It was true, the sun was sparkling and dancing on the waves.

"I've never swimmed in the sea," he said a little nervously.

"Never?" said Warren.

"No. Dad says the sea is for fishes."

Mrs. Troll flicked off a wasp that was crawling up her thigh. "That's because he's frighted of water."

"I am not!" growled Mr. Troll indignantly.

"You are, Eggy. You never go near it. Not since that time you got butted off a bridge by a billy goat."

Mr. Troll scowled. He didn't see the point of the seaside. There was nothing to chase and no one to roar at.

Mr. Priddle adjusted the waist of his swimsuit and took a few deep breaths. "The best way is to run straight in," he advised Ulrik. "Don't paddle in the shallows. Just take a deep breath and dive in. Copy me and you'll be fine."

"Okay, I'll try," nodded Ulrik.

They ran down the beach. Ulrik was the first to reach the water and splashed in excitedly. A wave broke over his knees as he plunged in deeper. The water was as cold as ice. Mr. Priddle jumped up and down shouting, "Ahhh! Heee! Ha-hooo!"

"Ahhh! Heee! Ha-hoooo!" repeated Ulrik, anxious to do everything correctly. They were up to their waists now. Mr. Priddle stretched out his arms and flapped them as if he were a pigeon preparing for take off. "Oh! Oh my!" he gasped, but the rest was lost as a huge wave crashed over all three of them and Ulrik got a mouthful of salt-water. When he could see again, he found he was on his own. Mr. Priddle was wading back rapidly toward the beach, spluttering and coughing. Ulrik splashed after him excitedly. "Uggsome!" he called. "Did you see me? I swimmed!"

Back on the beach they found Mrs. Troll performing an odd kind of dance. She shook her

head, flapped her arms violently, and slapped at her thighs.

"Do you have to do that?" complained Mrs. Priddle. "You're kicking sand on me."

"I can't help it," said Mrs. Troll. "It's these buzzlebees—they're everywhere!'

Mrs. Priddle put down her book. A cloud of insects hovered over Mrs. Troll, buzzing angrily.

"They're not bees, they're wasps!" she yelped, leaping to her feet.

"Wisps?" said Mrs. Troll.

"Wasps! Where did they come from?"

"I don't know," said Mrs. Troll, swatting the air furiously. "But I wish they'd go back."

Mrs. Priddle noticed the yellow drips running down Mrs. Troll's legs.

"What on earth is that?" she pointed.

"Sunscreen."

Mrs. Priddle saw the empty yellow tube lying on the sand and seized it. "Wait! You didn't use this?"

"Yes, it was in the bag."

"Not the picnic bag! That's mayonnaise! It's meant for the sandwiches!"

"What?" gasped Mrs. Troll.

She rushed off toward the sea with the angry wasps buzzing after her. On the way she passed Ulrik, who stopped to watch his mom plunge into the waves, flapping her arms above her head. For a beginner, she seemed to be getting the hang of swimming.

Ten minutes later, Mrs. Troll sat shivering on the sand with a beach towel wrapped around her.

"How are you feeling now?" asked Mr. Troll, sitting down beside her.

"Sore," said Mrs. Troll. "I've been stinged all over."

Mr. Troll sniffed her shoulder. "You still smell stinksome," he said.

"Thank you, my lugly," said Mrs. Troll.

Warren and Ulrik had been trying to play soccer but the tide was coming in and the ball kept going in the sea.

"Mom, I'm hungry! Can't we get ice cream?" whined Warren.

"I think that's a very good idea," said Mrs. Priddle. "Why don't we all go to the café and have a nice cup of tea?"

Sunny Bay Café was a small wooden building just down the hill from the parking lot. Considering it was the peak of summer, the café didn't seem to be very busy. The only customers were an elderly couple drinking coffee at a table in the corner. When they saw Mr. Troll duck his head to squeeze through the door, they banged down their cups and rose from their seats in alarm. The man spilled some coins on the table and they bolted for the exit, almost knocking over the Priddles in their haste.

"Well! Really!" said Mrs. Priddle.

"Why does everyone run off as soon as we arrive?" asked Ulrik.

"They didn't even finish their lunch," said Mr. Troll. He helped himself to a half-eaten doughnut and licked the sugar off his fingers.

Mrs. Troll looked around the empty café. Under a glass case was a tempting display of cakes, pies, and tarts, but there was no one to serve them. A coffee machine coughed and gurgled by itself.

"That's funny," she said. "There's nobody here."

"Yes, there is," said Ulrik.

"Where?"

"Over there." Ulrik dropped his voice to a whisper. "I think she's playing Hide and Sneak." He pointed under one of the tables and they all bent down to look. A middle-aged woman in an apron was trying to sneak out on her hands and knees toward the kitchen door. Ulrik crept over and bent down until his face was level with hers.

"FOUND YOU!" he cried.

The woman jumped, banging her head on the table. She crept out and smoothed her apron into place.

"What do you want?" she asked, edging behind the counter rather nervously.

"Four nice creams," said Mr. Troll. "And Mrs. Piddle wants the potty."

"He means a pot of tea," said Mrs. Priddle, turning pink.

"Yes," said Mr. Troll. "And what kind of pie is that?" He pointed to the largest one.

"Apple," said the woman.

"Oh," said Mr. Troll, disappointed. "I was hoping it might be goat."

The woman introduced herself as Mrs. Evans and brought the tea and ice cream to their table on a tray. After the first shock of seeing the Trolls, the color had returned to her cheeks.

"You gave me a fright, walking in like that," she said. "I'd just been reading that terrible article in this morning's paper."

"What article was that?" asked Mr. Priddle, pouring his wife some tea.

"You haven't read it?" asked Mrs. Evans.

"No."

"But surely you must have heard?"

"Heard what?" said Mrs. Priddle.

"Well . . . about the beast." Mrs. Evans picked up the *Aberduffy Herald* from the next table and held up the front page for them to see.

"BEAST STRIKES AGAIN!" ran the headline in big, bold letters.

Mr. Priddle took the paper and started to read. "Good gravy!" he said, and a moment later, "Good gracious!"

"For heaven's sake, Roger, what does it say?" cried his wife impatiently.

Mr. Priddle read the article out loud. *"Late last night the Beast of Boggy Moor struck again. Eyewitnesses report hearing 'strange sounds' coming from the moor after midnight. A dozen sheep have disappeared, bringing the number of attacks this month to four."*

"Attacks?" gasped Mrs. Priddle.

"Police have asked the public to remain calm," her husband went on. *"'We are following a number of lines of inquiry,' said Sergeant Morgan of Aberduffy police. 'Anyone with any information should remember there is a $500 reward for the capture of this beast.'"*

"Wow! Five hundred dollars!" repeated Warren. He exchanged looks with Ulrik, remembering their puzzling conversation with Farmer Ogwen. No wonder he'd warned them to keep off the moor.

Mrs. Priddle set down her teacup. "What do you

mean by beast?" she asked nervously. "What kind of beast?"

"Ah, that nobody knows," said Mrs. Evans, drawing up a chair to sit down. "No one's ever gotten close enough to say. There've been several sightings in the last month. All late at night, and all on the moor."

She lowered her voice and they all leaned closer to listen. "Mrs. Price saw it one night when her car broke down on her way back from Advanced Yoga. There's an evening class in the village hall on—"

"Never mind that! What did she see?" Mr. Priddle interrupted.

"Oh, yes. She was terrified. Really shaken up. It passed by not a hundred yards from her car."

"What was it like?" asked Warren.

"Like a wolf, she said. Or maybe a werewolf—with burning eyes and savage teeth." She turned to look at Mr. Troll. "In fact, a bit like you."

"Me?"

"Yes," said Mrs. Evans. "You weren't out on the moor late last night?"

"Don't be silly," said Mrs. Troll. "We only arrived yesterday and Eggy was asleep with me."

"That's true. We heard him snoring," said Mr. Priddle.

"Still," said Mrs. Priddle, "it explains a lot."

"What do you mean?" asked Mrs. Troll.

"Well, that's why people run away when they see you. They think you're this dreadful beast creature."

"But what about the sheeps?" Ulrik wanted to know.

Mrs. Evans looked at him. "That's the strangest part. You'd think there'd be blood and bones, wouldn't you? But there's never any trace. It's like they've been swallowed whole. A hundred sheep in the last month. I ask you, what kind of beast has that kind of an appetite?" She sat back and smiled pleasantly. "So how's the tea? Shall I bring you another slice of apple pie?"

Mrs. Priddle shook her head. "Actually," she said, "I'm not feeling all that hungry."

A Darksome Night

THAT evening, the two families sat in the camper, talking. It was past eleven o'clock but nobody had mentioned going to bed. The truth was they felt safer in one room. The lamp cast long shadows, and the gas fire hissed softly. Steam rose from their mugs of hot chocolate.

"Why didn't Ogwen warn us? That's what I'd like to know," said Mrs. Priddle.

"Maybe he didn't want to alarm us," suggested her husband.

Ulrik had been thinking back to the morning. "He did sort of warn us. He told us to keep off the moor, didn't he, Warren?"

"Yes," agreed Warren, eager to have an opinion. "But he didn't tell us why. I thought he was just trying to scare us."

"Huh! He managed that all right," said Mrs. Priddle bitterly. "No wonder there are no other campers. It's hardly a tourist attraction—a wild beast prowling the moor, devouring sheep."

Mr. Troll hadn't spoken for a while. He was staring intently out of the window. Suddenly he held up a finger. "Shhh!"

Everyone fell silent.

"What?" whispered Mr. Priddle.

"That noise. Can you hear it?"

They listened again. The camper rocked slightly. Nobody moved for a full minute.

"What kind of noise?" whispered Mr. Priddle at last.

"That strange moaning noise. Like 'Ooooooooh! Ooooooooh!'"

"You mean like the wind moaning?"

Mr. Troll listened again and his expression relaxed. "Oh yes, it's only the wind."

Everyone let out a groan. "Please don't do that!" said Mrs. Priddle irritably. "My nerves are on edge as it is. Maybe we should all go to bed."

Warren shook his head. Now that it was dark, he wasn't feeling quite so brave.

"What if it comes tonight?" he said. "What if it tries to get in?"

"I'm sure it won't, Warren. We'll lock the door."

"But maybe it's a ghost. Ghosts can walk through doors."

"That's true," said Mr. Troll. "I once heard of a headless goblin—"

"PLEASE! Don't talk about goblins!" shouted Mrs. Priddle, banging her mug down on the table.

"Sorry," said Mr. Troll. "I was only going to say I've got an idea."

"Oh Lord!" groaned Mr. Priddle.

"I was thinking, why doesn't one of us stay on guard? Then we'll all be as safe as mouses."

"Actually, it's not a bad idea," admitted Mr. Priddle. "But who's going to stand out there in the dark?" They all looked at each other.

"I will," said Mr. Troll. "I'm not frighted of hairy beasts."

Mrs. Troll leaned over and gave him a kiss. "You're my big hairy beast," she said.

"Well, that's settled then," said Mrs. Priddle. "Egbert can stay on guard while the rest of us try to get some sleep."

Ulrik turned to his dad, as the others got ready for bed.

"Dad, can I be on guard with you? I won't be frighted," he said.

Mr. Troll smiled and ruffled his son's hairy head. "Of course you can, my ugglesome."

Outside, Mr. Troll stamped his feet and blew into his hands to keep warm.

"You stay here, Ulrik, while I go and look for some firewood. A nice roaring fire will keep us warm."

"Can't I come with you?" asked Ulrik.

"No, somebody's got to stay on guard. I won't be long."

Ulrik nodded doubtfully.

"Remember, what are trolls?" asked Mr. Troll.

"Fierce and scaresome."

"That's right. And what do trolls do?"

"They roar. Rarrgghh!" growled Ulrik, pulling his fiercest face.

"Not bad," said Mr. Troll, patting him on the head. "If you hear anything, give a roar and I'll be here in two shakes of a goat's tail. All right?"

Ulrik nodded again. His dad strode off into the darkness in the direction of the woods, leaving him alone. He hugged himself and bounced up and down to keep warm. It was a cold, blustery night with inky clouds racing across the moon. Actually, he hadn't told the truth about not feeling scared. With his dad around he felt safe, but he hadn't expected to be left by himself in the dark. Trolls weren't scared of the dark, of course, but it wasn't the dark that worried him, it was what was *out there* in the dark.

The light in the camper suddenly went out, leaving him with only the moon and stars for company. He wished his dad would hurry up with that firewood. How long had he been gone now? The wind gusted and the camper shuddered on the steep hill. Ulrik tried to think of something to take his mind off being scared. Maybe he could start building the fire. That would impress his dad. He knew the first thing to do was to make a circle of stones or rocks, so the flames wouldn't set fire to trees or campers. Luckily, he found just what he needed close at hand. Propped against the wheels of the camper, he found four heavy rocks. It was almost as if someone had left them there on purpose. Surely no one would mind if he borrowed them for a bit? He began to drag them out one at a time. When he was almost finished, something made him look up—the soft thud of footsteps in the dark. They were coming closer.

"Dad?" Ulrik croaked. "Da-aaad?"

"Baaaa!" said the something. A fat sheep trotted out of the dark, followed a moment later by Mr. Troll, clutching an armful of sticks.

Before long, Ulrik was warming himself in

front of a crackling fire. The wood was a little damp, but it soon caught and started to burn. Mr. Troll was impressed with the rock circle Ulrik had made.

"Just what we needed," he said. "Where did you find them?"

"Under the camper. Someone must have left them there."

"I didn't know Piddle collected rocks."

"Neither did I," said Ulrik. The gusting wind blew the smoke in his eyes so he had to look away. The camper groaned and rocked on the hill. It gave a sudden lurch.

"I used to collect rocks when I was your age," Mr. Troll was saying.

"Dad!" said Ulrik, grabbing his arm.

"Me and Snorvik used to trade them—"

"Dad!" interrupted Ulrik. "The camper!"

Mr. Troll turned around just in time to see the camper slip past him. It was parked at the top of a steep hill, and the slope was taking effect. Slowly at first—like an ocean liner heading out to sea—the camper began to drift downhill. It swayed and bumped over the grass and picked up a little speed.

Ulrik and Mr. Troll chased behind, shouting useful advice like, "Stop! Come back!" but the camper took no notice. Even when Ulrik caught up and tried to hang on to the back, it dragged him along until he lost his grip and fell over.

Inside, Mr. Priddle had awoken with the first sudden jolt. At first he couldn't remember where he was, then he remembered he was warm and safe in his camper. Except that something was wrong. The camper was bumping and rattling as if it were caught in a hurricane. Sitting up, he saw the farmhouse drift past the side window. Strange, he thought—farmhouses don't usually do that. Unless . . .

"JACKIE! WARREN! WAKE UP!" he bellowed.

His wife grunted. Warren rolled onto his side.

"We're moving! Wake up!"

Mrs. Priddle's eyes blinked open. A glass rolled past her line of vision, followed by the bedside table sliding past. She sat bolt upright.

"Roger! We're moving!" she shouted.

"I know!"

"But how?"

"Never mind how! Let's get out before it's too late."

Mrs. Priddle dragged Warren protesting from the bed. The three of them stumbled and slid in their panic to reach the door. The floor was listing like the deck of a ship in a storm. The fridge door swung open, spilling out milk and eggs and turning the floor into an ice rink. Warren stepped

on a strawberry yogurt and fell back on the bed, which gave a twang and folded beneath him. To add to the confusion, Mrs. Troll burst out of her bedroom in her pink nightgown, roaring at the top of her voice. The camper, meanwhile, hurtled downhill at an alarming speed, its wheels spinning like a yellow Ferrari. Suddenly there was a bang, followed by an almighty splash as it ran out of the field. They bobbed around for a moment, listening to bubbling, glugging sounds. Mr. Priddle was the first to grasp the situation.

"The pond! We're sinking!" he cried.

"We're going to drown!" wailed Warren.

Mrs. Troll pushed past him and wrenched the door open with an effort. A flood of water gushed in over her feet. She grabbed Mrs. Priddle by the arm and pulled her to the open door. "Jump!" she urged.

"Jump! Jump!" cried Mr. Priddle.

Mrs. Priddle jumped. She landed in cold, murky brown water up to her waist. It was full of weeds—and other things. She slopped her way to the bank in her silk pajamas and sat down among the reeds.

Moments later, Ulrik and Mr. Troll arrived at the pond out of breath. Mr. Troll watched the camper rapidly sinking as water flooded in the door. His wife was wading to the bank, carrying Warren piggyback.

Mr. Troll shook his head and whistled softly.

"Thank uggness!" he said. "That could have been nasty."

A Bit of a Temper

THEY all spent the night in the old barn, sleeping on bales of hay. It was drafty, uncomfortable, and smelly, with a roof that leaked when it started to rain. At seven o'clock they were awakened by Ogwen and his dogs, coming to take the sheep out to the field. Mrs. Priddle opened her eyes to find the toothless farmer grinning down at her.

"Morning!" said Ogwen cheerfully. "I hope you slept well."

"Not really," groaned Mrs. Priddle. Her back

ached. Everything ached. Her best silk pajamas were sopping wet. All her dry clothes were in the suitcase, which was in the camper—which had sunk to the bottom of a filthy pond. It was hard to see how this vacation could get much worse.

The others emerged from the mountain of hay, yawning and dusting themselves off. Farmer Ogwen took in their bedraggled appearance and chuckled.

"Been for a midnight swim, have you?"

"We had an accident. Our camper ran away," explained Mr. Priddle.

"I know, I've seen it," said Ogwen, shaking his head. "You're going to need a tractor to pull that out. You should have left the brakes on."

"Yes. Why didn't you, Roger?" asked Mrs. Priddle coldly.

"I did. I think they need fixing," said Mr. Priddle. "But I'm sure I wedged some rocks against the wheels. I remember doing it."

"Oh," said Ulrik, so loudly that everyone turned to look at him.

"What do you mean, 'Oh?'" asked Mr. Priddle.

Ulrik looked at his feet sheepishly. He had a feeling he was in trouble.

Later that morning they all gathered around the pond to watch Ogwen attempt to rescue the sunken camper. The muddy water came up to the bottom of the windows. Ogwen waded in up to his waist, trailing a thick rope behind him. He fished around in the water until he had located the towbar. Once the

rope was securely attached, he waded back to the bank, climbed into the cab of his red tractor, and revved the engine.

The camper came out with a loud sucking noise, like a hippo emerging from a mud bath. Water gushed out of the door in a brown waterfall, bringing with it a lampshade, three cans of sweet corn, and a soggy roll of toilet paper. Thick, smelly mud oozed off the wheels and clung to the sides.

"It will be fine once we've cleaned it out," said Mr. Priddle hopefully.

"Fine?" said Mrs. Priddle. "FINE?"

"Well, maybe a little damp."

"Look at it, Roger! It's filthy! It will stink for days."

Mr. Troll stuck his head in between them. "We don't mind the stink," he said.

Mrs. Priddle gave him a severe look and yanked her husband to one side so they could speak in private. She lowered her voice.

"Roger, I've tried," she said. "I've tried to put up with them. But there comes a point when it's asking too much. They'll have to go. Make up your mind—it's either them or me."

The Trolls stood side by side watching the tractor tow the dripping camper back up the hill. Mr. Priddle approached them and cleared his throat awkwardly.

"Ah, Piddle," said Mr. Troll, turning around. "Everything's all right, then?"

It was the wrong thing to say. Even Mr. Troll saw that when Mrs. Priddle's eyes bulged like a toad's.

"All right?" she burst out. "All right? You turn up here and ruin our vacation! You sleep in our beds and eat all our food! And, as if that's not enough, last night you tried to drown us!"

"'You're having a tantrum," observed Mr. Troll.

"I know I'm having a tantrum!" shouted Mrs. Priddle.

"That's okay, trolls have tantrums. I roar when I'm having a tantrum. It makes you feel better."

"I don't want to roar," glared Mrs. Priddle. "I just want you to take your things and go!"

Mr. and Mrs. Troll looked at each other and back at the Priddles. "Go?"

"Yes—go!"

Mrs. Troll blinked. "But we were just starting to enjoy ourselves."

"In case you hadn't noticed, *I* am not enjoying myself," said Mrs. Priddle. "I am cold, wet, and miserable."

"And having a tantrum," added Mr. Troll helpfully.

"But where can we go?" asked Mrs. Troll.

"I don't care! Anywhere! Find a hotel, a bus shelter—anything you like as long as it's not near us."

Mr. Troll rubbed his snout. "So we're not on vacation anymore?"

"Not with us, you're not!" thundered Mrs. Priddle, who stalked off up the hill with her husband following meekly behind. The Trolls stared after them, at a loss.

"Well! For uggness' sake!" sighed Mrs. Troll.

"Yes," agreed Mr. Troll. "Imagine getting all hot and blethered over a tiddly bit of water."

"It was quite a lot of water," admitted Mrs. Troll. "But you know what peeples are like."

Her husband nodded. "Crazy as a sack of goblins."

"And just when I thought we were all getting on so well," said Mrs. Troll. "What are we going to do now, Eggy? Where are we going to sleep tonight?"

Mr. Troll frowned. "I don't know. Where's Ulrik?"

They looked around. There was no sign of him. Warren stood with his back to the barn and his hands covering his eyes. He seemed to be counting to himself.

"Ahh! They're playing a game!" said Mrs. Troll. "Why don't we leave them, Eggy? There's no sense in upsetting Ulrik now. We can come back for him once we've found somewheres to sleep."

"All right," agreed Mr. Troll. "You think there might be caves?"

"You never know."

"Come on, my lugly."

Mr. Troll took his wife's hand and together they set off toward the village.

Hide and Sneak

"...**F**ORTY-NINE, fifty!" Warren opened his eyes. Actually, he hadn't kept them fully closed. He'd been peeking through his fingers the whole time in order to see where Ulrik went. Just as he suspected, Ulrik had made a beeline for the woods, since there wasn't really anywhere else on the farm to hide. It wouldn't take long to find him, though Warren wasn't in a big hurry.

The woods were dark and they backed onto Boggy Moor. Warren wasn't scared himself, of course. All the same, as he entered the woods, he stopped to arm himself with a big stick.

He followed a rough, muddy path and eventually came to a wide clearing overgrown with ferns. Looking around, he half expected to see Ulrik's large hairy head or his bottom poking out from behind one of the trees. There was no sign of him. Warren went on, swishing at the tops of the ferns with his stick. *Swish!* Ogwen had warned them to stay out of the woods, he recalled. There wasn't anything to worry about, of course—the beast only came out after dark. *Swish, swish!* Though you could never be certain. It might be here watching him right now.

He halted and glanced around nervously. Maybe if he hadn't stopped, he wouldn't have noticed the odd way the ferns lay on the ground ahead of him— as if someone had arranged them deliberately. He prodded one aside with his stick. Underneath was a piece of chicken wire, and beneath that a dark, yawning hole. Warren squatted down to examine it more closely. It was some kind of animal trap, and if he'd taken a couple more steps, he would have fallen right into it! But why would someone dig a hole in the middle of the woods? It was far too big for catching rabbits, and he hadn't come across any other wild animals.

The words in yesterday's paper jumped into his mind—"$500 reward for catching the beast." So that was it! Someone was after the reward! Warren almost wished he'd thought of the idea himself. Five hundred dollars was a lot of pocket money—think of all the candy and ice cream he could buy with that! He pictured his photo on the front page of tomorrow's paper and his name in the headlines. They'd call him "Warren the Beast Slayer."

Of course, it was only a daydream. He was never going to catch the beast or get his hands on the reward . . . unless . . . A sly smile spread across Warren's face. Nobody actually knew what the beast looked like, did they?

Carefully, he replaced the ferns so that the hole was hidden from sight. Once he was satisfied, he stood up and raised his hands to his mouth.

"ULRIK! Ulrik, over here!"

Ulrik, meanwhile, was getting tired of hiding.

He'd been crouching in the middle of a prickly bush for what felt like hours. One of his feet had gone to sleep. Maybe Warren had given up looking for him altogether. Maybe he was too scared to come into the woods. He pricked up his ears. Someone was shouting his name.

He followed the voice until he came to a wide clearing, where he found Warren waiting for him.

"Why didn't you come to find me?" he asked.

Warren shrugged. "I've been looking. You're too good at hiding."

Ulrik looked pleased. "Really? Does that mean I winned the game?"

"Yep, you won. Come on, let's go back now." Warren sounded impatient.

"But isn't it your turn to hide?" asked Ulrik.

Warren glanced down. One more step. "What?" he said.

"I said, 'Isn't it your turn?'"

"No! The game's over. Hurry up!"

"Oh. I thought . . ." But Ulrik never got to say what he thought because, as he took another step toward Warren, the ground suddenly gave way beneath his feet. He fell into the trap, with branches and ferns crashing down on top of him.

For a moment he lay still, more dazed than hurt.

"What happened?" he groaned.

Warren peered down at him. "Looks like you fell in a hole."

Ulrik scrambled to his feet. He'd bruised his knee. The hole was so deep that even standing on his tiptoes he couldn't reach the top. He stretched up a hand to Warren.

"Help me out!"

Warren shook his head. "I can't."

"Warren!"

"Sorry, you're too heavy. You weigh a ton. If I try to pull you out, I'll probably end up falling in with you. Then we'll both be stuck."

Ulrik blinked up at him. It was true, he was bigger and heavier than Warren.

"What are we going to do?" he asked anxiously.

"Don't worry, you stay there. I'll go and get help."

"Wait!" called Ulrik. "You're going to leave me all by myself?"

"It won't be for long. I'll run back to the camper and tell them what's happened. Five minutes and I'll be back again."

"You promise?"

"Scout's honor," said Warren, raising a hand in salute. He gave Ulrik a cheery wave and walked away, smiling secretly to himself. He had never been in the Scouts, but Ulrik didn't know that.

Missing Ulrik

BACK at the farm, Mr. Priddle was doing his best to clean out the waterlogged camper. He squeezed muddy brown water from his mop into a bucket. His wife and son were refusing to help—Mrs. Priddle said they were on strike. She looked up from the novel she was reading and shook her head.

"I don't know why you're wasting time on that, Roger."

"The floor's almost dry," said her husband.

"I've told you, I'm not sleeping in there."

"You'll get used to the smell after a while."

"I don't want to get used to it. I want to move to a nice hotel."

Warren stopped juggling his soccer ball. "Will the hotel have a swimming pool?" he asked.

"Of course it will, my dear," said Mrs. Priddle.

Mr. Priddle thumped his mop on the floor. "We're not going to any hotel, we're staying here! I've paid Ogwen for two weeks!"

"Fine. You stay in your smelly old camper if you like, Roger. We won't," said Mrs. Priddle, placidly turning her page.

Mr. Priddle emptied a bucketful of brown water into the grass. "The sun's shining, you're out in the fresh air, what more do you want?" he asked.

Mrs. Priddle gave him a withering look. "Dry clothes," she said.

"Can I have cooked breakfast at the hotel?" asked Warren.

"Have what you like, darling, your father's paying," said Mrs. Priddle.

"Will the Trolls be coming too?"

"No," said Mrs. Priddle firmly. "They're having their own vacation."

"Where?" asked Warren.

"I have no idea. That's up to them."

Warren glanced anxiously back at the woods. It was hours since he'd left Ulrik and set off toward town with the intention of claiming the $500 reward. But the closer he got to the village, the more he'd begun to lose faith in his plan. For one thing, he wasn't exactly sure where the police station was. For another, he doubted the police would believe a word of his story. Hairy and ugly he might be, but Ulrik didn't sound much like a savage beast once he opened his mouth. He was far too gentle and good-natured. Even worse, Warren thought, what if Mr. and Mrs. Troll discovered that he'd tried to swap their son for $500? Warren had seen Mr. Troll get mad and he didn't wish to be picked up and swung around by his ears. No, he'd decided in the end, it would never work. Far safer to go back and just keep quiet.

When he returned to the camper, his parents were too busy arguing to even notice that Ulrik was missing. All the same, Warren was starting to feel uneasy. What if Ulrik never got out of the hole? What if he stayed there forever and starved to death? Come to think of it, Warren was pretty hungry himself. Wasn't it time for supper?

His dad carried a bundle of soggy sheets from the camper and began to hang them on a clothesline. "I wonder where they are," he pondered.

"Who?" asked his wife.

"The Trolls. They've been gone for hours. You think they're all right?"

"All right?" snorted Mrs. Priddle. "They're trolls, Roger, not children!"

"Yes," said Mr. Priddle. "That's what worries me."

Mr. and Mrs. Troll's search for somewhere to stay was not going well. As soon as the villagers saw them coming down the hill, they scurried into their houses and locked their doors. Mrs. Troll spotted a sign in the window of a tall white house offering "Bed and Breakfast," but when she knocked on the door a hand appeared and turned the sign around so that it said "No Vacancies."

"Now what?" she asked her husband.

Mr. Troll pointed down the hill to a van parked by a playground.

"Look! There's a camper just like the Piddles'."

When they got closer, they found the camper was empty. It was bright pink, and for reasons Mr. Troll didn't fully grasp, it had a giant ice-cream cone parked on the roof. People's strange ideas never ceased to amaze him. He peered in through the window. "It's a bit tiddly," he said, "but we could all squish on the floor."

"I don't know, Eggy," said Mrs. Troll doubtfully. "Doesn't it belong to someone? Maybe we should ask."

Mr. Troll looked up and down the deserted village street. "Who can we ask? Come on, they won't mind if we take a look. Give me a legs-up."

Mrs. Troll panted and pushed him from behind while her husband struggled to squeeze his bulky frame through the narrow window.

"Push harder!" said Mr. Troll. "My bottoms are stuck!"

"I am pushing harder! You've put on weight!"

"One more shove!"

Mrs. Troll summoned all her strength and gave one last shove. It did the trick, and Mr. Troll fell head-first into the van, grabbing at a lever to try and break his fall. A large blob of ice cream oozed from a nozzle. It hung for a moment and then landed neatly on top of his head. He scrambled to his feet.

Mrs. Troll stared at him. "A bird's plopped on your head."

Mr. Troll dabbed at the blob with a finger and tasted it. "That's not bird-plop, it's nice cream,"

he said. "Ulrik will love this—a camper with its own nice cream."

He then helped his wife in through the window, and the two of them inspected their new lodgings.

"It's much tiddlier than the Piddles'," said Mrs. Troll. "Where's the folding bed?"

She opened a door. A blast of cold air hit her in the face and mist billowed out. "It's full of candy," she said.

"'Scuse me!"

A shrill voice brought Mr. Troll to the window. A small, curly-haired girl was staring up at him, holding out a coin.

"A Ninety-nine, please, mister," she said.

"Pardon?" replied Mr. Troll.

"A Ninety-nine. With chocolate flakes."

Mr. Troll turned to his wife. "She wants ninety-nine chocolate cakes."

"We haven't got any cakes."

"I know. Maybe she'll take a nice cream instead."

"Wait there," he told the little girl. He examined the ice-cream machine and pulled down the lever. A large blob of whipped vanilla plopped on the floor between his feet. Mr. Troll tried again and managed to catch the next blob on his right foot. He looked around for a bowl or plate, but there didn't seem to be any. Instead he raised his foot and propped it carefully on the counter. "There we are. One nice cream," he said. "You'll have to lick it off." The little girl frowned back at him.

Just then, a voice made them look up. A man was running down the hill toward them at high speed, his white coat flapping behind him.

"Hey!" he shouted angrily. "What do you think you're doing?"

"Bogles!" muttered Mr. Troll.

"I told you we should have asked," said Mrs. Troll.

"That's my van! Get out of there!" bellowed the man.

"I think it's his camper," sighed Mr. Troll.

"Yes," said Mrs. Troll. "And it doesn't look like he wants us to stay."

Half an hour later, the Trolls arrived back at the farm. By now the sun was low in the sky and the shadows were lengthening. They had spent most of the day wandering the road between the village and Sunny Bay. Now they were returning, weary and homeless. "What are we going to tell Ulrik?" asked Mrs. Troll gloomily.

Mr. Troll shrugged. "Maybe the Piddles will have changed their mind. Maybe they'll let us sleep with them tonight."

Mrs. Troll shook her head. "I don't think so. Mrs. Piddle was having a big temper."

"Yes," agreed Mr. Troll. "Peeples look funny when they're having a temper. Their faces go red as tomatoes. Does mine do that?"

"No, my lugly, it stays green."

They found the Priddles by their camper. Mr. Priddle had dragged all the mattresses outside and was attempting to dry off the damp patches with a hairdryer. Mrs. Priddle watched him with her arms folded and an impatient expression on her face. She didn't seem overjoyed to see the Trolls back again.

"Well?" she said.

"We tried everywhere," said Mrs. Troll. "No one wants us to stay."

"I can't say I blame them," said Mrs. Priddle.

Mrs. Troll looked around. 'Where's Ulrik?'

"Ulrik?" Mr. Priddle blinked in surprise. "I thought he was with you."

"No," said Mrs. Troll. "We left him with you. He was playing with Warren."

They all turned to look at Warren, whose cheeks had gone so red that Mr. Troll wondered if he was having a tantrum.

"Warren? Have you seen Ulrik?" asked Mrs. Priddle.

"Um . . . well, I saw him a while ago," admitted Warren. "But then he went off."

"Off? Off where, for uggness' sake?" demanded Mr. Troll.

Warren avoided his gaze. "I don't know. He didn't really say."

Mrs. Troll looked at Mr. Troll. "Oh, Eggy! It's not like Ulrik to go off without telling anyone. What if he's lost? What if something's happened?"

"Now, now, let's all try to stay calm," said Mr. Troll, pacing up and down and looking anything but calm.

Mrs. Priddle turned to her son. "Warren, try to remember. This is important. Which way did Ulrik go?"

Warren bit his lip. If he said the woods, they would find Ulrik trapped in the hole and everyone would blame him. Better to put them off the scent. He frowned, pretending to think, then pointed up the hill.

"That way."

Mrs. Troll clasped a hand to her mouth. "Eggy! The moor! He's out on the moor!"

Troll in the Hole

ULRIK hugged his knees and shivered. Darkness was closing in and he could see the moon pale as a ghost overhead. He'd lost track of how long he'd been trapped in the hole. At first he'd thought it was only a matter of time before his mom or dad would find him, but hours had passed and no rescue had come. Surely by now Warren would have told them what had happened?

He'd given up trying to escape—the hole was too deep and the sides too muddy and slippery to climb. His voice was hoarse from shouting for help. All he could do was wait and hope that someone would find him. He hummed to himself, trying to remember a trollaby[1] his mom used to sing to him as a troggler. Mrs. Evans had said the beast came out after dark. Surely it wouldn't want to eat a plump young troll? Sheeps were much more tastesome. Abruptly he stopped humming. What was that? Had he imagined it? That awful howl carried on the wind? He listened. A second howl split the night air, this time longer and louder than the first.

Ulrik tried not to panic. If he stayed where he was, maybe the beast would pass by. But what if it didn't? What if it smelled him? Dogs could pick up your scent and maybe beasts were the same. He reached up, making one last desperate attempt to escape. His fingers touched something hard and he grabbed at it. Warren's stick fell into the hole at his feet.

Half a mile away, Mr. Troll climbed on top of a rock and cupped his hands to his mouth. "ULRIK!" he roared. "Ul-rik!"

---

[1] Trollaby—soft crooning song, often about hunting goats.

There was no answer. Mr. Priddle shone his flashlight into the dark. "It's no use," he said. "We'll never find him out here."

The moor seemed to be endless. Craggy rocks loomed in the dark like giants, and solid ground gave way to boggy marsh that squelched under their feet. Mrs. Troll blew her snout loudly into her hanky. "My poor little Ulrik!" she sniffed.

Warren dug his hands in his pockets and shivered. "Can't we go back now?" he begged. "There's nothing out here."

"You go back if you're frighted," said Mr. Troll. "I'm not giving up till I find him."

"Me neither," said Mrs. Troll. But before they could go on, they heard a sound that chilled them to the bone. It was the same bloodcurdling howl that Ulrik had heard in the woods.

"Jumping goblins!" said Mr. Troll.

"That's not a goblin," said Mr. Priddle. "It's some kind of animal. It came from the woods."

A low moan escaped from Warren's mouth.

Mr. Priddle shone his flashlight on his son's face, which had gone deathly white.

"It was only a joke," Warren stammered. "I thought he'd be all right. I never meant . . ."

"What the bogles is he blethering about?" growled Mr. Troll.

"Ulrik," babbled Warren. "He fell down a hole in the woods. It was an accident!"

"What?" said Mr. Priddle. "Why on earth didn't you say this before?"

Warren whimpered. "I thought you'd be mad!"

"I am mad!" shouted Mr. Priddle.

"I'm double mad!" roared Mr. Troll. "I'm mad as a mad hatter!"

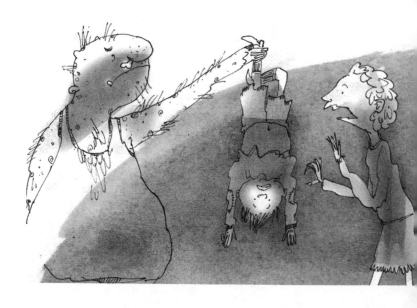

Before anyone could stop him, he seized Warren and dangled him upside down by one leg.

"Arghhhhh!" shrieked Warren. "Daaad!"

"For uggness' sake, Eggy, put him down!" scolded Mrs. Troll. "It's Ulrik we need to worry about. He's all alone in that wood with a scaresome beast!"

"By the bogles, you're right!" said Mr. Troll, dropping Warren in a puddle. "We've got to find Ulrik before it's too late! Come on!"

He set off, bounding toward the woods at great speed with the others trying to keep up.

Beastly!

BACK in the hole, Ulrik was certain the beast could smell him. Just now he'd glimpsed a pair of huge yellow eyes moving through the trees like searchlights. A menacing growl made his hair stand on end and reminded him that he wanted to go to the bathroom. He gripped his stick tightly. If the beast came at him, he decided, he'd poke it in the eye. Or maybe it would be better to throw the stick and shout, "Fetch!"—he'd seen that work on a dog once.

A rustle in the trees told him the beast was

approaching. He shrank back in the shadows of the hole. Heavy footsteps came closer. Whatever it was, it was big enough to make the ground shake. A shadow loomed over him and a bright light dazzled his eyes. Ulrik jabbed upward with his stick.

"Owwww!" yelped Mr. Priddle.

"Ulrik?" said a familiar voice. "Is that you?"

"Dad!" cried Ulrik.

Mr. Troll's strong arms reached down and caught him, lifting him out.

His mom wiped away a tear and hugged him so tightly he could hardly breathe. "Thank uggness! Are you all right, my ugglesome?"

"I'm fine," said Ulrik.

"He poked me in the eye!" complained Mr. Priddle.

"Sorry, I thought you were the beast," said Ulrik. "I heard it!"

As if on cue, another growl came from the moor.

"Good gravy!" gasped Mr. Priddle, forgetting his sore eye. "That sounded close!"

Warren tugged at his dad's sleeve.

"Let's go back!" he begged. "Mom will be getting worried."

Ulrik held up a hand for silence. "Listen!" he said.

They all heard it—a faint bleating carried on the wind.

"Sheeps," said Mr. Troll.

Warren panicked. "It's coming for them!" he trembled. "It's after the sheeps—I mean sheep."

"But, Dad," said Ulrik, "we can't just leave them. They'll be eaten by the beast."

"They won't be the only ones if we don't get out of here," muttered Mr. Priddle.

But he was talking to himself—the Trolls were already creeping forward through the trees, toward the moor and whatever was out there.

Ulrik peered out from behind a tree at the edge of the woods. He could see the beast's dark head over the top of a stone wall. His mom and dad crept forward to join him.

"Ready?" whispered Mr. Troll.

Ulrik and Mrs. Troll nodded.

"No roaring," hissed Mr. Troll. "Let's take it by surprises."

"You're the one who's always roaring," said Mrs. Troll sniffily.

"Shhh!" said Ulrik, gripping his stick.

"After three," said Mr. Troll. "One, two, three . . ."

The Trolls came running out of the woods and threw themselves on top of the beast. Ulrik leapt on its back and grabbed it around the neck. It toppled over limply. Something funny had happened to its growls, which sounded like someone gargling underwater. Ulrik let go and sat up, staring in surprise.

"Good goblins!" said Mr. Troll. "It's just a dog."

The black Labrador lay on its side, staring ahead with glassy eyes. It had been stuffed and mounted on wheels like a pull-along toy. Under the dog's belly were two speakers, from which came the deafening growls and howls they'd heard earlier. Someone, it seemed, had been playing a trick.

A hundred yards down the slope, the headlights of a truck lit up the moor. Ulrik realized that this was the pair of yellow eyes he thought he'd seen from the woods. The driver turned off the engine and got out, closing the door. Even from this distance Ulrik recognised the baggy trousers and shabby coat.

"Look! It's Ogwen!" he whispered.

"Good gravy! So it is!" Now that the fighting was over, the Priddles had joined them. The five of them crouched in the dark to watch. Ogwen put his fingers to his mouth and whistled to his dogs. Fang and Claw were rounding up a small flock of confused-looking sheep and chasing them toward the back of the truck. In a few minutes, the farmer had them all inside and bolted the tailgate shut. Ogwen gave another shrill whistle, calling in his dogs.

"I don't believe it," hissed Mr. Priddle. "He's a rustler!"

"A wrestler?" Mr. Troll looked puzzled.

"He's stealing them, Dad. They're not his sheep," explained Ulrik.

"Great goblins! You mean he's a robber?"

"Yes!"

Mr. Troll bunched his fists and rose to his feet. There was nothing he hated more than robbers. "Wait till I catch him!" he threatened. "I'll tromp on his bellies. I'll swing him by the uncles!"

Ulrik pulled him back. "Wait, Dad. I've got a better idea."

"Better than tromping?"

"Yes. Let's see how *he* likes getting a fright."

Ogwen closed the door of his truck and grinned toothlessly. He was pleased with his night's work. Twenty-three more sheep to add to his growing flock. At this rate, he'd soon be the richest farmer in Aberduffy.

He returned to the edge of the woods, where he'd left Bessie. It was amazing what you could do with a stuffed dog and a few sound effects. At the edge of the woods he stopped and looked around, baffled. The dog was gone! Vanished! But that was impossible—how could it walk off by itself?

"Grarrgghh!" A loud roar from the darkness startled him. It wasn't like the growls and howls on the tape—this sounded all too real and alive.

"Who's there?" he asked, trying to steady his quavering voice.

The reply was a second roar, this time coming from somewhere closer to the truck. His escape was cut off. Ogwen backed away toward the trees, trembling. There was more than one of them—maybe a whole pack of wolves or bears closing in on him.

"GRARRGH!" The next roar was so loud he yelped and crashed through the woods, ducking under branches. Scratched and panting, he came out into a clearing. Something was standing there waiting for him. When he got closer, he saw it was Bessie, her glassy eyes shining in the dark.

"Bessie?" he said uncertainly.

"Grrrrr!" replied the dog. Ogwen's mouth gaped open.

"Bessie? Is that you, girl?"

"Grrrrrr—robber—grrrrr!"

Ogwen pinched himself. Was he dreaming? The dog had spoken to him, calling him a robber. But Bessie had died five years ago. Maybe it was her ghost, returning to haunt him.

"Bessie, it's me, Olwen! It's your master!" He reached out a hand cautiously.

"GRARGHHH!" roared Ulrik, leaping out from behind the dog.

"Arghhhhhh!" yelled Ogwen as the ground gave way and he fell back into the deep, muddy hole.

When he came to his senses, he saw three hairy trolls grinning down at him from above.

"Well done, Ulrik!" said Mr. Troll. "That was fun!"

"Did I make a good dog? Grrrr!" said Ulrik, showing his fangs.

Mrs. Troll patted him proudly on the head. "You were scaresome, my hairling."

A short time later, Sergeant Morgan arrived from the local police station.

"Hello?" he said, shining his flashlight. "I heard there was some trouble. We had a call from a Mrs. Puddle."

"Priddle," said Mr. Priddle wearily.

"Pardon?"

"Priddle. That's my name."

"Oh. Who's this in the hole?" He shone his torch on the miserable face of Ogwen. "Olwen Ogwen. Well, well! What are you doing down there?"

"He's a robber," Mr. Troll informed the sergeant. "He's been wrestling sheep."

"Wrestling them?"

"He means rustling," explained Mr. Priddle. "If you look on the moor, you'll find his truck. The stolen sheep are in the back."

"And this," said Ulrik, "is the beast of Boggy

Moor." He trundled Bessie forward so that the policeman could see her and switched on the tape. Growls and howls came from the two speakers. Sergeant Morgan took off his cap and scratched his head.

"Well, I'll be jiggered! So that's what it was! The chief's going to be pleased about this. Very pleased. We've been trying to get to the bottom of this for months. Of course, I never believed in all this beast nonsense myself."

"Didn't you?" asked Mr. Priddle.

"Oh no, not for a moment. 'Someone's leading us on a wild goose chase'—that's what I said to the chief. So it turned out to be Olwen Ogwen all the time! Imagine that! There'll be a reward for this, you know."

Mr. Priddle's face brightened. "A reward? Goodness! I had no idea."

He felt a large hairy hand on his shoulder. "Ahem!" growled Mr. Troll.

"Oh, well, yes," said Mr. Priddle hastily. "Strictly speaking it was Ulrik who did most of the work."

Ulrik smiled shyly as the sergeant shook him firmly by the hand. "Good work, young Ulrik. You come by the station and we'll see about that five hundred dollars, shall we?"

"Uggsome!" said Ulrik.

A loud groan made them all look around. "Are you okay, Warren?" asked Ulrik. "You've gone a bit green."

Wish You Were Here!

MRS. PRIDDLE lay on her beach chair and sipped her fruity cocktail through a straw. The ice cubes clinked soothingly against the glass. Below her balcony, she could hear children laughing and playing happily in the hotel swimming pool. Warren's shrill voice rang out above the hubbub. "Mom! Watch me!"

Mrs. Priddle waved back at him. "Lovely, darling! Well done!"

She sighed deeply—at last, a real vacation! The strange events of the previous night seemed like a dream. In any case, everything had worked out well. After hours of tramping through the moor, Mr. Priddle was ready to abandon his damp camper and move into a comfortable hotel. She glanced at him now, lying on the beach chair next to hers.

"So there never was any beast at all?" she said.

"Mmm? No. I told you, Ogwen invented the whole thing just to keep people off the moor at night."

"But what about the story in the paper? People claimed they saw it."

Mr. Priddle chuckled. "It just shows you the power of the imagination. Tell people there's a savage beast on the moor and that's what they believe. Actually, it was nothing more than a stuffed dog—Ogwen's favorite Labrador, Bessie. It seems he couldn't bear to be parted from her."

"Heavens! He sounds like a total fruitcake," remarked Mrs. Priddle.

"I'm afraid so. I heard him tell the police the dog had come back to haunt him."

Mrs. Priddle shook her head. She had never trusted the farmer from the start—you could tell he didn't clean his teeth well.

"Well, thank goodness it's all over," she said. "No more sleepless nights, no more campers, and best of all, no more trolls."

"Bliss!" agreed Mr. Priddle.

Mrs. Priddle closed her eyes, hoping to doze off. She could hear seagulls calling and the *putt-putt* of a car coming slowly along the road. Actually, it didn't sound like a car, it was more like . . .

"Oh, good gravy!" said Mr. Priddle, sitting bolt upright.

"What?"

"That's our camper!"

"Don't be ridiculous, Roger. We left it back at the farm."

"It is, and it's turning in here!"

Mrs. Priddle's eyes snapped open and she jumped to her feet. Below her balcony, she could see a large red tractor turning into the drive. At the wheel was Mr. Troll, who had never driven a tractor before but was obviously enjoying the experience. He was towing the Priddles' battered old camper behind him, and Ulrik and Mrs. Troll were hanging out of the windows.

"Oh, no!" groaned Mrs. Priddle. She tried to hide but it was too late—Mr. Troll had spotted them and waved excitedly.

"Piddle! Look what I've got. We've cleaned it up for you!"

"Cleaned it up?' Mrs. Priddle turned pale. She didn't want to think what that meant.

Mr. Priddle waved his arms. "No! We don't want it! Go away!"

"What?" asked Mr. Troll, putting a hand to his ear and forgetting to steer. The tractor swerved violently to the left.

"I said . . . look out!" shouted Mr. Priddle.

The tractor plowed straight across the Hotel Majestic's lawn, leaving deep muddy tracks in its wake. It was heading directly for the swimming pool. Sunbathers ran for cover, scattering in all directions. A waiter dropped his tray of drinks and vaulted a beach chair faster than an Olympic hurdler. The pool was emptying fast.

"Brakes!" bellowed Mr. Priddle. "Use the brakes!"

"Which one is brakes?" Mr. Troll called back. He had only just learned how to make the tractor go forward—stopping it was another matter. He chose a lever at random and pushed it, jamming his foot down on one of the pedals. The tractor leaped forward like a startled kangaroo. The Priddles shut their eyes, unable to watch. When the splash

came, it was so enormous that it drenched them even though they were five floors up.

Bubbling and hissing, the tractor went down in the deep end, dragging the camper in with it. A moment later, Ulrik bobbed to the surface, followed by Mr. and Mrs. Troll. They struggled to the side of the pool, where a crowd of spectators had gathered to watch.

Ulrik climbed up the steps and sat down.

"Mom! Did you see me? I swimmed!"

"Well done, my ugglesome!"

The manager of the Majestic pushed his way through the crowd, crimson with rage.

"Is this your camper?" he demanded, pointing to the sunken wreck.

The Trolls looked at each other. "Well, no," said Mr. Troll. "It isn't."

"Then whose is it?"

"It's the Piddles'."

Mr. Troll pointed to the balcony—but strangely enough, there was no sign of the Priddles at all.